1,000 Words

1,000 Words

AN ANTHOLOGY OF TERROR

Goe

Contents

1

Gifts from Afar

When I stuck my hand in the black gift bag sitting on the table, I couldn't help but let my mind swirl with ideas on what was inside. Charlotte and I always exchange the most interesting gifts from our travels, and this time she said she found the one thing that would top all the others. Naturally, my curiosity was peaked when she said that while she boarded the plane to return home from Mexico. I stretched out my fingers around the object lying in the bottom of the bag. It felt cool and smooth but had ridges all around. I gripped the mystery gift and slowly pulled my arm back out feeling the weight of the present resist the motion. Charlotte's eyes were wide with excitement watching me examine the strangely beautiful memento she bought for me. My eyes scanned over the item in my hand taking note of each and every detail, the bleached white surface broken up by the squiggles of deep cuts of black, the hollowed-out eye sockets decorated with tiny rivers of red paint, the too-long grin stretched across the bottom dotted with tiny pointed yellowed teeth. The thing was wonderfully grotesque, and my eyes lit up as my mind processed the unique gift given to me.

"This is amazing." I finally uttered out, my words filled with wonderment and fascination.

"I knew you'd like it. I came across a village while exploring the area," she began to give me the story, "and there was a woman there dressed in all dark, but very traditional looking clothing. She waved me over to look over her table. When I saw this off on the side, I asked her how much it'd be. She looked at me in a very curious way but told me the price, so I traded the pesos and picked it up."

I couldn't stop staring at the decorated skull in my hands, there was something drawing my attention so deeply that I barely heard Charlotte's story.

"But there's something weird I should tell you." Her face turned to a confused, solemn expression. "The woman told me you have to welcome each day to it when you first wake up, and good nights before you go to sleep." Charlotte's eyes stared into mine as if to make sure I heard her correctly. Of course, I snickered, but in the back of my mind something told me she wasn't joking.

That night after returning home, I set the beautifully decorated skull on the nightstand next to the bed. It seemed to almost glow in the darkness that surrounded it. I watched some terrible horror movie, had a nightcap, brushed my teeth, and made my way to bed. As I lay in the darkness, Charlotte's words echoed in my mind, and my eyes flew open. With no seriousness at all, I lolled my head toward the skull on the nightstand and whispered, "Good night to you," before drifting off to sleep.

In the morning, I woke up from a well-rested sleep and jokingly spoke to the skull, "Good morning, skully." I rolled my eyes and snickered at my actions, but there was still a thought in my mind about 'what would happen if I didn't do it?' Nothing note-worthy about my Saturday happened, just the normal run of errands, house chores, and budget balancing. While I changed my bed sheets, I looked over at the skull and thought it looked slightly different than before. The smile seemed to be more crowded, almost as if another tooth had pushed its way through. Clearly it had only been in my possession for a night, so I likely just hadn't gotten used to it yet.

Over the next few days, I skipped out on a 'good morning' or 'good night' here and there, but nothing happened. I'm not sure what I expected if I didn't greet my foreign gift, but the thought that *something* would happen was kind of exciting. I turned in for the night, lay on my side facing the skull, and stared at it. My brow furled as I realized there was a hole in the mouth. Was that there before and I didn't notice? It looked like a tooth had popped out. I ran my hand over the surface of the nightstand but couldn't find any fallen pieces. "Hmm." And I took a deep breath, closed my eyes, and drifted off to sleep.

The next day I looked at the skull Charlotte had given me again; another tooth had gone missing. I couldn't believe it. Where were they going? How were they falling out? I couldn't understand the strange event. As normal, I brushed my teeth after I showered, but I noticed a slight pain in the back of my mouth when the bristles brushed over my teeth. I rinsed my mouth out and opened it wide, trying to look into the back through the mirror but I didn't see anything. "Probably another damned cavity." I told myself.

Over the course of the next week, several more teeth went missing from the skull. I had texted Charlotte about the strange happening, and she simply asked if I had been saying good morning and good night like she told me. "Are you kidding me? You really think greeting the damn thing keeps it together? The old lady was probably just trying to spook you." I texted her back.

I had a dentist appointment on Tuesday morning, my mouth was sore than ever, so I figured it was time to have a professional check. They took a couple x-rays and came in to review them with me. He hung the transparent copy up on the lightbox and flicked the switch on. My eyes widened with fear. He looked over at me with a concerned expression and said, "I've never seen this before, but you're growing teeth."

That night before I fell asleep, I looked at the skull and said, "Good night. I'm sorry."

The smile grew.

11

Mirror, Mirror

Aidan stared at his reflection in the dirty, broken mirror in the bathroom. The blood was smeared across his entire face, dark rivers of red streamed down his cheeks, twisting at the crevices of his face, and dripping off his sharp chin. His eyes were wild, bewildered from the terrifying being staring back at him. His body continued convulsing from the jolts of electricity his nerves shot through his muscles. His deep brown eyes appeared to be black, soulless. The shard of glass was still in his hand, digging deeper into the open cut it had created, but he couldn't loosen his grip. He could feel the warm, thick threads of blood trailing down his body under his shredded t-shirt. The lines were seeping through the light-yellow shirt tinging it with dark splotches, but there was nothing Aidan could do to stop the bleeding. He was no longer in control of himself, rather the reflection of himself.

Three days ago, Aidan's entire world crumbled around him;

his wife left him for his estranged brother, his career was halted by sudden layoffs, his bank account had been hijacked and nearly drained, and his house was being foreclosed on for non-payments which was managed by his wife. Aidan did his best to take each blow life issued him, but he didn't see an end in sight, and he began to break down.

At first, he closed himself in his home office and let his mind shut down. He tore the room to pieces, yanking books off the shelves and throwing them across the room, pulling the desk drawers out and dumping their contents on the floor, smashing picture frames with his fist, and ripping the lamp from the socket to heave it at the door. His breath was ragged when he fell to his knees in the center of the 10-by-10-foot square room in the middle of the chaotic storm that had just occurred.

That night, Aidan couldn't sleep at all. He kept tossing and turning, looking at the red alarm clock numbers that taunted him by not moving fast enough. Eventually he grabbed the clock and whipped it across the bedroom. Another sleepless 30-minute interval, and Aidan left the bed altogether. He caught his reflection in the closet door's mirror and saw the heavy bags already growing under his eyes. He moved away from the horrible figure staring back at him, not noticing it remained in the mirror as he left the room.

The next day is when he received the call from the bank informing him there had been suspicious activity in his account, and they needed him to meet with a banker immediately. Not showered, wearing the same torn t-shirt he had on the night before, and his dark brown hair twisted this way and that, Aidan walked into the bank like a living zombie. He sat with a woman named Sarah who was clearly trying not to notice his appearance and listened to her explain all the issues with the account. Foreign charges, multiple debits at the same stores, transfers from his account to an unknown one, the list was endless. That's when the well put together Sarah broke the news that a woman by the name of Presley Cauffield had emptied and closed the savings account, leaving with nearly $8,000. His soon-to-be ex-wife had wiped him clean. Sarah suggested closing the current account, so Aidan took the $422.19 out in cash and left the bank. On the drive home, he looked up in the rearview mirror and saw the anger growing behind his eyes. Was that his reflection? He hardly recognized himself. The dark eyes gleamed back at him as his own gaze refocused on the road ahead of him.

Expecting another restless night, Aidan lay on the couch and listened to the whir of the ceiling fan. The familiar sound was strangely soothing. His eyelids began to get heavy, but before they closed for the night, he looked into the glass patio doors in front of him seeing his reflection. As he succumbed to the heaviness of slumber's calling, the reflection stood from the couch.

Aidan opened his eyes to a deeply dark space. As soon as his body left the couch, it vanished into the darkness. He took a few confused steps forward searching for anything familiar, a door, a table, his house. *Where am I?* His arms outstretched in front of him as he fumbled around the dark, unsure of his surroundings.

"You can't handle all this, Aidan." A voice spoke from the darkness, his voice.

"Wh-who's there?" He called out, panic sinking into his own voice.

"Let me out, Aidan. It's time for me to handle the situation.

I'll make everything right again." The mysterious voice was easily identified as his own, but it wasn't coming from his mouth.

Admitting defeat, Aidan responded, "It's all so bad. So, so bad."

"I'll take care of it for you, just say the words and I can be released from this place. But you have to say you want everything fixed. You have to be the one to release me."

Aidan dropped to his knees, the stress of everything weighing on his shoulders too much to handle. In a half whimper, he spoke to the strange voice that sounded exactly like him. "I want everything fixed."

The news reporter outside the police car holding the bloodied Aidan announced into the camera, "Tonight, a madman has been apprehended by local authorities after he went on a rampage killing not only his own brother and wife, but several coworkers, a banker in the downtown branch, and seriously wounding several others in between each location." The camera moved to show Aidan sitting in the back of the police car, head hanging low. "When asked why he went on this seemingly chaotic storm of killing, he responded: the mirror man told me he'd fix everything."

Aidan looked at his reflection in the window and smiled at his deranged mirror twin.

111

One Wish

It has been three days now. Three days without seeing another living creature, no birds, no dogs, no spiders, and worst of all, no people. Kevin continued driving around the abandoned streets of his town where nothing seemed out of place other than the fact there wasn't a single person anywhere to be seen. There wasn't some massive car pileup or any kind of radioactive leak from the factory, there weren't any mass murders that took place or alien invasions. There was no media coverage to refer to and seek answers from, there weren't any television programs now. Kevin wandered the desolate country-burb town of Pinkerton all on his own confused at how everyone in town could have just vanished without a trace. He slowly drove past the town square where many locals had opened up shops for baked goods, breakfast restaurants, local art, hardware stores, handmade clothing, and grocery stores which people shopped and mingled, gossiped with their neighbors about who was doing what where, and where kids would window-shop along the pavement deciding on how much of their allowance they were really willing to spend for a new toy or the latest sneakers. This center of community and togetherness was now a barren wasteland, where in just three days dust already began to settle on empty countertops, natural hardwood floors, and silent windowsills. Lights were left on, doors unlocked as if someone reached into the town like a dollhouse and removed the occupants in mid-task. He blew his car horn, shouting out the window for anyone to answer him, but he was only met with the echo of his own voice and even that seemed to him so far away. *An entire community doesn't just go missing.* Kevin thought to himself as he stared out in the distance for any sign of life, but knowing he'd never see anyone ever again.

At seventeen years old, Kevin thought he had it all planned out; he was going to become a famous writer, head to college for a formal education in writing and literature, publish his first book by the age of twenty-five, find a good place to live far from his po-dunk, small-minded town and never look back. The people of this town didn't understand his writing, they couldn't grasp his complex emotional massacres or the demons he invented in his mind and put down on the paper. They labeled him as disturbed, mad, and a freak. They outcasted him from local artist showcase events at the library or county fairs. To Kevin, the entire town was against him and his talent, and when it came down to it, he knew the best way to resolve his isolation was to remove himself from the situation.

Three days ago, Kevin drove to his favorite get-away-from-it-all spot under a bridge near the edge of town. Frustrated with the latest round of criticism he received after reading an excerpt from his latest horror story to the librarians, he parked his car off the side of the road and stomped down the gravel and dirt path which led to the small stream under the bridge. He plopped down against the old stone wall and fumed with rage. *Not every fucking story needs to be about some dumbass farmgirl who falls in love with some idiot farmboy where they live happily ever fucking after!* The voice in his head was screaming. He picked up a few rocks and chucked them across the small stream of flowing water, bouncing them off the other wall of the old bridge. The sound echoed between the hollow space and splashed against the gentle water moving near his feet.

"One day. One bloody fucking day these asinine people will regret not supporting me." He growled aloud through gritted teeth. Kevin continued spewing rocks across the empty space in front of him, allowing the anger to subside through releasing it. He wasn't disturbed he thought. He just enjoyed horror stories from the likes of Poe, Lovecraft, Stoker, and Rice. He adored the brutes they created and would get lost in the tales they told of misunderstood monsters, dangerous psychopathic minds, and murderous madmen. It didn't make him a psychopath or dangerous, it's art and he appreciated the tales for what they were. *One day.* He thought in his head again.

Some time had passed, maybe an hour or two, when Kevin began feeling less enraged, and so he stood up and dusted off the dirt from his jeans, ready to return to town and self-isolate in his room for the umpteenth day in a row. Just as he was leaving the bridge's protection from the blistering farming sun, he heard the faintest whisper reach out and tickle his ear. He turned around and stared into the dimly lit bridge, seeking the source of the whisper. Not seeing anything moving or hearing anything callout again, he assumed it was just a voice in his head. He spun on his heels and took another step away from his sanctuary.

"Oooonnnneeee wiiiiisssshhhh..." the raspy whisper of a voice swirled around Kevin's head like a warm spring breeze through the treetops. Kevin spun around again sure he'd find someone nearby, but looked bewildered when he was met with an empty cave of a bridge. He stepped back under the bridge, but still nothing was in front of him. Kevin stood very still listening for the voice to return, but he could only hear the gentle babble of the stream. He closed his eyes and took a deep breath.

"Oooonnnneeee wiiiiisssshhhh..." The voice filled the space under the bridge and Kevin's eyes flew open. He scanned the dark area, his protection from the outside world, but no one was there.

"One wish?" He asked the mysterious, invisible whisper. His eyes looked down at the ground as he retreated to his mind. Bringing his eyes up, and biting the inside of his lip, he spoke with a tinge of anger. "I wish everyone would just disappear."

IV

The Last Dance

Randy was no stranger to a foggy night given the bog at the bottom of the hill on his property. The fog was always thickest during the cold nights in the fall when the insect chatter is minimal, the frogs don't hop as often, and the turtles have taken shelter in the deeper parts of the bog. Through the wall of windows that made up his back porch, Randy could look out over the hillside and the seemingly endless rows of trees past the bog. He'd sit in his favorite lounger with his cozy slippers on, a warm cup of tea by his side, and a flannel blanket over his knees and watch as nightfall swallowed the woods. He would watch the fog rise slowly from the bog, taking shape and consistency as the night's air cooled across the land. It would slowly creep up the weathered trunks of the forest's trees and level out, by his estimate, around 12 feet. Now and then a deer would emerge from the forest creating an eerie silhouette against the fog. Randy's mind loved playing tricks on him, making believe an otherworldly creature was sneaking out of its hiding place, exploring the surrounding area.

The old country home had survived years of storms, whirlwinds from small twisters, sheets of rain, harsh winters that froze the land, and blistering heatwaves from the summer's sun. Randy built the house with his wife when they were first married, but that is a distant memory now. He survived his wife, but there was never a day that passed when he didn't think of her. He could remember the gentle rose-scented perfume she wore and how it tickled his nose when she'd rest her head against his chest, the way she would wake up an hour ahead of him to do her hair even though she was beautiful no matter what condition her hair was in, and he thought often of her smile that lit the darkest of rooms. Randy frequently wished he had just one more chance to twirl his late wife on the dance floor, her powder blue dress swirling around her calves as they tightly held their hands together ensuring her safe return to his loving arms. Nearly every night, the couple would sit side by side in their matching hers and his chairs and watch the moon rise over the blanket of trees, and even without her next to him, it was a habit he had no intention of breaking.

Tonight, the fog rolled in as expected and hid the grassy hillside, the overgrown bog, and the messy branch-covered forest floor. As Randy sipped his tea, he saw a shadow emerge from the forest. He had just realized that the shadow had appeared every night for the last few days. He always assumed it was just another deer, but tonight the figure took on a clearer shape. A familiar shape. He set his warm mug of tea on the side table and sat up in the cozy chair, leaning forward toward the wall of windows. He tried to focus on the strangely familiar silhouette in the distance, picking up his glasses to get a clearer image. Just as his wrinkled hands finished fumbling with the pair of lenses and secured them on the bridge of his nose, the silhouette evaporated and vanished back into the forest. Randy let out a sigh of disappointment and sat back in his chair.

The next night, he decided to watch the fog from the back garden, once beautifully blooming with bright colored flowers and luscious leaves of green, but now overgrown with yellowing weeds and tangled vines. He sat on the rickety wooden bench bundled up in his warmest coat and the flannel blanket lying across his legs and waited. The night grew darker, the moon rose, the clouds opened to a sea of stars, and finally the fog began to rise. Randy stared toward the wall of trees, longing for the shape from the night before to return. Just when he was about to return to the warmth of his home before freezing over, a darkness began forming in the middle of the trees, inching closer to the edge of the forest. The dark mass took shape, but this time he was ready with his glasses waiting on his forehead. He slid them lower and as his eyes readjusted to the clearer image, a small quick gasp escaped his mouth. The silhouette took form, the same familiar shape as before, and Randy instantly recognized it as his late wife's shape.

He stared at the ghostly shadow of his wife in pure astonishment, tears bubbling to the edges of his eyes, burning from the coolness of the fall's night air. The figure stepped forward and fully took shape. A powder blue dress, sinched at the waist and held tight against the body, the bottom pleats billowing from the slow movement as she stepped closer toward Randy. He stood, letting the blanket fall to the garden, and began walking toward this impossible image in front of him. They met halfway, his eyes searched the shadow figure and slowly her facial features began taking shape. He reached out for her hand and when it met his, they began slowly dancing. Years of aches and pains washed away from his body, suddenly he felt as if he was 26 years old again, twirling around the thick fog with his beautiful wife.

She twirled away from him, their hands locked in each other's as they used to, and then she began returning toward him. Randy's eyes were closed, using muscle memory to dance with his wife again. When he felt her returning to his body, he opened his eyes. The dress swirled around her calves, and as her face returned to his, it twisted into a horrible, dark fanged creature with blood-red eyes. Just as he was about to scream, the creature's jaw unhinged and swallowed him whole.

Death embraces us all.

V

～

The Nothingness

Bernie hated the dark. No, he despised the dark. He detested the nighttime because it meant there was no safe place to hide from the shadows that grew from the deepest of corners, spreading their tentacles of shade across the floor, up the walls, stretching to the ceiling where they writhed back and forth through the moonlight filtering in from the tree's twisted branches. The dark was the worst place Bernie could imagine and it all started twenty-one years ago when he was 6 years old.

Bernie's dad had passed away early in his life, so most memories he has are from photos or videos his mom shared with him. He learned later in life his dad suffered from paranoid schizophrenia, his mom explaining it had developed over time, and he'd been getting treated for the disease since his early 30's. There had been good and bad days, but she admitted to always having a belief that one day his mental state would take her husband away. The only actual memory Bernie has of his father is one that sticks with him day in and day out, it shook the young boy to his core and thinking of it now still sends a shiver down his back.

Darnell burst into Bernie's room one night, frantically shouting, shocking his young son awake from a sound sleep. His dad held a flashlight in his hand and blinded him when he sat up in bed, tears already welling in his eyes of fright. Darnell ran to him and said, "Don't worry, son. I won't let them take you." Then he scooped the 6-year-old up in his arms and rushed out of the room. He shoved his son into the backseat of the car and began driving down the long dirt driveway which led to the country road. He turned all the interior lights on and was speaking in gibberish, frantically looking out each of the windows, his eyes wild with fear. Bernie remembers crying in the backseat of the car, screaming for his mommy. When they reached the end of the drive, the black paved country road stared back at the car with a menacing gleam which caused Darnell to stop abruptly, tossing Bernie forward, hitting his head on the front passenger seat. The next thing Bernie can remember is watching his screaming father be ripped out of the car by long black shadowy tentacles just before his mom swung the back door open and rescued her terrified son.

It's taken several trips to a children's psychologist and more than his fair share of medical tests, but Bernie finally came to the realization that so much of that memory is fuzzy and disconnected from reality because of his young age and the trauma he had been through. Even knowing that events of that night are nothing more than a pseudomemory, he can't help recalling it time and time again. Bernie has woken up screaming in his bed drenched in sweat with a racing heart, clenched fists wrinkling his sheets. He practices his coping exercises and focuses on moving forward, but the dark is always around him. Clawing at the floorboards when he walks past a shaded corner, taunting him from darkened rooms before he flicks the light on, and reaching for him from under the refrigerator.

Bernie bought his first house and began the tedious task of packing his apartment up and unpacking it all in the new bungalow. It was a great starter house with an open floorplan, plenty of windows for natural light to filter in, a finished basement, natural hardwood floors, and fully equipped with motion-sensor lights all around the outside of the house. If he's truly honest with himself, that's what sold the home to him. After unpacking several of the boxes, he decided to store them in the attic. He opened the door leading to the narrow staircase and stared up at the darkened top, a shiver wriggling its way down his spine. He flicked the light on and felt better about heading up the stairs. As he climbed up, the single light bulb hanging from the rafters began flickering, so he quickened his pace. The light from the bulb hardly sufficed for the size of the space, so most of the attic was pitch black. No windows or skylights, not even a vent where some of the afternoon's light could beam in were up here. Bernie took a gulp and held his breath as he stepped toward the storage area to leave the empty boxes. As he lay the boxes down, he heard a creak in the floorboards echo from the darkest part of the attic. Bernie twisted his head toward the sound staring into the nothingness with eyes bulging from their sockets, he could both feel and hear his heartbeat racing inside his chest.

Bernie wanted to run, but his body was frozen in fear; he stood in the light's edge trembling with terror. The bulb continued to flicker in and out. In between the flickers, he noticed a mass of a shadow appear to be moving closer to him from the nothingness ahead. His eyes widened, his lip trembled, his hands shaking at his sides. Between each of the flickers, the mass took another step closer to petrified man staring in disbelief.

A tear welled in Bernie's eye and slid down his dark, smooth cheek before dropping to the dusty attic floor. The shape transformed, became clearer as it neared him. Standing in front of Bernie not three feet away was his father, staring back at his now grown son. His eyes looked sorrowful and apologetic. Bernie couldn't stop himself from wondering if his father had passed his disease to him – this had to be an illusion.

Darnell took a step forward and spoke to his son, "I can't stop them from taking you, too."

The light flickered out. Shadowy hands reached from the floor, grabbed Bernie's legs, and pulled him down into the nothingness.

VI

The Surfer's Secret

Living in a surfer town was one of Karlie's top goals in life ever since she watched shows like *Summerland* and *Blue Water High*. She dreamed of sunny days, warm sand under her toes, and exciting times with friends catching waves all day long. She always felt like she didn't fit in with anyone in her town of Deadwood. With a name like Deadwood, you can only imagine how much surfing took place.

Karlie dreamed of white sandy beaches, bright blue waters, and surfing on a pink and white board riding the waves like a champion. Even though she had never surfed before, there was something inside her that yearned for the water like a calling deep in her soul. That call was finally answered the day her mom returned home from work and said they were going on a vacation to Santa Cruz. Karlie nearly fainted from the news! She was finally going to get her chance to be surrounded by the beach-going teens she'd be dreaming of meeting.

Once Karlie and her mom reached their California destination, Karlie's eyes were stuck open wide taking in all the breathtaking views of the ocean, colorful buildings, the eccentric energy running through the population, and all the smells from vendors lined on the boardwalk waiting for hungry customers. It was exactly as she had dreamt, even more than she imagined. Karlie's mom decided to go to a spa, but she was only interested in being at the beach, so her mom allowed her 16-year-old daughter to dream away, but she had two rules. The first rule was to stay on the beach outside the resort they were staying at, and the second was to stay out of the water. Karlie objected to the water rule, but her mom gave her the ultimatum of following the rules or not leaving the room, so reluctantly she agreed to the guidelines as is.

Karlie dug her feet into the warm, white sand and allowed herself a moment to soak it all in. She wandered the beach, walking up and down the water's edge, watching the surfers in the distance, the kids swimming close to the coastline, and speedboats zooming by near the horizon line. Before long, she came across a group of girls around her age sitting together conversing and laughing with their bleach-blonde hair flailing in the wind, their sun-kissed bodies shimmering from the bright sun. They were just like the girls in her favorite shows and movies. She nervously walked over to the group, deciding this might be her only chance to meet people like this.

She approached the five girls, forced out a smile, and greeted them while introducing herself. The girls responded immediately, taking in the fair-skinned, dark-haired friendly stranger. They all introduced themselves and quickly became friends with Karlie. They shared stories of where they grew up, what life at the beach was really like – it wasn't quite as true as the television shows Karlie watched – all their hobbies, shared interests, and whatever else came up. Before long, the sun had started to set, and the group of girls invited Karlie to a sundown bonfire across the beach where they were planning on meeting up with friends, boyfriends, and other teens to chat with. Before she even thought about asking her mom, she agreed to the gathering.

At the bonfire, there was music, and someone was grilling, there was plenty of water and juices to stay hydrated, and Karlie didn't want to be anywhere else in the world. She met a very nice guy, quite easy on the eyes, who chatted with her most of the time. The guy's name was Chance, and she found herself batting her eyelashes before too long, lusting after his soft green eyes and dimpled smile. They decided to take a walk down to the coastline, a few yards from the fire and the group of teenagers.

"I can't believe you've never been surfing before. I think I was on a board by the time I was six or seven." He chuckled at Karlie's misfortune (in his eyes).

"I've never been in the water before. My mom always stops me." She admitted under a bashful glance at the tanned boy walking so close to her that their arms kept brushing against each other.

"That's insane!" He suddenly stopped and faced her; his eyes were filled with disbelief. "Come on, I'm going to teach you right now." He grabbed her hand and together they ran over to a couple of boards standing in the sand further down the coast.

Karlie was scared, she didn't want to embarrass herself, but she also didn't want to disappoint Chance. She stood at the water's edge and watched him paddle away from her, biting her lip, she called out to him. "I have to tell you something!" But he couldn't hear her. She took a deep breath and closed her eyes. Before she opened them again, she took the first step into the water.

Chance looked back toward the coastline, ready to call for Karlie to join him, but she was gone. Over the ebb and flow of the waves, he saw her dark hair against her pale body paddling towards him. He let out a smile, glad she was joining him finally. A wave came, and she disappeared. It went, and she reappeared. Another wave, and she disappeared. It went, and she was gone.

He sat up tall on his board searching for his new love interest but couldn't see her anywhere. Suddenly he felt a tug on ankle under the water. He looked down into the water, murky with the low light, and saw a flash of white. Before he could figure out what it was brushing against his legs, he saw the familiar dark hair rise from the water. Just then, Karlie's serpent tail wrapped around his legs, pulled him under, and she devoured him until nothing, but a surfboard was left bobbing in the water.

VII

Your Deepest Desire

Have you ever wished you possessed a superpower? Maybe something like the ability to fly or see through walls, the power to read minds or predict the future. Everyone's thought about it at some point in their life, usually as a child after reading their first superhero comic or watching a riveting movie featuring supernatural humans. Everyone wants to be something bigger than they are, the belief that if they focus hard enough, they can teleport from city to city in the blink of an eye, or perhaps move things with their mind alone. Certainly, Scarlett Gibberson dreamed of possessing a superhuman ability. And with determination, strong emotions, and enough motivation she discovered an ability inside her soul, or at least an ability that possessed her soul.

Scarlett floated through life on her own dark cloud. She never excelled in school, rather passed enough to move forward, she didn't have a strong circle of friends from the constant relocations her parents put her through, and she isolated herself in her bedroom to keep her parents from judging her preferred style of clothing. Scarlett learned early in life that she was a fall leaf in a winter storm, destined to be alone and ride on the season's wind until she found her place to crumble. Many of the kids in her school labeled her as a goth, witch, or freak, but she kept her head down and continued coasting through life, attempting to be as unseen as possible.

Reading was her true sanctuary where the world was plain and simple on black and white pages. She would allow the stories she read to consume her in a world of fantasy where people were accepted for who they were, held high in the minds of the people when they thought differently, and where literally anything could happen. Her favorite novels were centered around women who possessed powers – witches who cast powerful spells to get what they wanted, sorceresses who tantalized her enemies with dark magic, and sirens who sang beautiful songs to entrap their prey and feast on their obsessions. Scarlett would often finish these stories and then lay back against her dark sheets imagining a world where she had power. She didn't want to fly or see through objects; she wanted something simple and unnoticeable. She desired the ability to control things with her mind, not just things, but people; she wanted to dig her way into their brain like an earworm and change their behaviors. She always thought she'd use this ability to help change people's abhorrent behaviors, therefore making the world a slightly better place.

Scarlett's newest neighbor was, by far, the best neighbor she'd ever known. The woman was known to be a shut-in, a recluse who kept to herself, left only when positively necessary, and didn't speak to anyone. On some level, that sounded like a haven to Scarlett. She identified with this private lifestyle, admired the old woman without ever meeting her. She saw the dark, heavy curtains be yanked closed now and then as she returned home from school and wondered what kind of woman stood just outside her view. Scarlett would soon become the first person the local hag spoke to in nearly fifty years.

Another day full of odd looks, crude remarks, judgmental comments – this is what Scarlett called a typical school day. It was never only her fellow classmates either, it was from the people she passed on her walk to and from, or the teachers who thought she was out of earshot. It was from the small-minded cretins she had the misfortune of crossing paths with and who were found in every one of the suburban neighborhoods her parents forced her to occupy. As Scarlett approached the walkway to the well-manicured front yard her mother spent endless hours perfecting, she saw the old woman's curtain close. She stared at the aging house and decided to attempt to meet the local witch, so she turned on her heel and headed one house over.

Walking up the weedy yard's broken stone path, the area seemed to darken as she approached the door. Upon stepping onto the porch, the door creaked open to a dark foyer.

"Come in, my dear child." A sour, cackle of a voice called out to Scarlett. "Don't be afraid."

Scarlett took a step inside the creepy house shrouded in darkness, and once both feet were across the threshold, the door groaned on its hinges and closed behind her. A single dusty window above the staircase ahead of her allowed a sliver of light to fall across the old woman's face, wrinkled with age, one eye clouded over with a light blue tinge. She lowered her head ever so, stretching a weathered grin above her pointed chin. Scarlett took in a breath.

The old woman's dry, crinkled hands wrapped around Scarlett's neck much faster than humanly possible. Her eyes were wide and wild, she sucked in deep raspy breaths to take in Scarlett's scent. Suddenly a swirling mist encompassed the dark room, spinning around the two women, one ancient and one nubile. Scarlett's bright green eyes were wide in terror.

The old woman cackled out, sending an echo throughout the old wooden home, "Your deepest desire is what I will give. The price you will pay is for me to live." Both women's eyes widened to their fullest capacity before darkness swallowed the room.

The next morning, Scarlett woke up in her bed as the alarm clock rang. In her head she groaned, "Off." Silence.

As she made her way to the high school, she thought the man watering his yard and gawking at her should turn the hose on his face. And so, he did. The girls snickering at her should claw each other's eyes out. Their screams excited her. Scarlett had just realized what power she now possessed. She stood in front of the school and glared at it with devious eyes – one green, and one cloudy blue.

VIII

The Woodlords

Local legend tells of a rotted dinizia tree in the forest that changes locations after you knock on it six times. If you knock on the tree, it will awaken the darkest Woodlord who will stalk you for six nights until you lead him back to his home in the tree. If by the sixth night you are unsuccessful, he'll drag you by a noose and hang you in the woods.

Grady and Brady are best friends who love ghost hunting, local legends, spooky stories, and everything that falls in that realm. Their shared interest brought them together during a local ghost tour when they were fifteen years old, and fifteen years later they still seek out the otherworldly apparitions together and travel around the world to follow local legends. All in the name of friendship and trying to be scared for life, so naturally when Brady heard of the Legend of the Woodlord, he called his best friend and made plans to travel to South America's Atlantic Forest.

The forest stretches across 1.5 million square kilometers in Brazil and is feared by all villages nearby. The thirty-year-old men made arrangements with a local guide who promised to take them into the forest, but only so far. He told them he can only go in as far as the light's edge, for if you go deeper than that, the Woodlords will find you.

"What exactly are the Woodlords?" Brady asked the Brazilian.

"They are keepers of the trees, protectors of the forest. Many will no bother you, you- uuh – not see them." His English was clear but broken. "They not see you as threat, leave you. But," his voice deepened, "if they think you there for bad reason, they will... lutar com honra, fight for they honor." The man's dark brown eyes stared into Grady's, then Brady's before he returned to a smiling face. "But you boys good, sim?"

With a snort, Grady answered back, "Sim. Yes, we're good."

The forest was much darker than they expected, and when their guide left them, the two men took a moment to take it all in. They began trekking deeper into the wooden area, stepping over huge leaves, hearing animals scurry about their business, listening to the sounds of the forest. They were following guides and suggestions they researched, but there was no clear way of locating the dinizia tree. After nearly two days of hiking, camping, and searching, the friends stumbled upon a dinizia tree with a massive hole exposing the middle. The tree was hollow, and from their view the tree matched the photos they found in their research. The two men approached the tree and looked at each other, confirming they were ready to knock. Grady faced the tree and clenched his fist. Brady followed suit, and together they each knocked on the hollow tree six times.

KNOCK... KNOCK... KNOCK... KNOCK... KNOCK... KNOCK

The men looked around the area, waiting for something to happen, but were only met with the familiar sounds of the forest they've listened to the last two days. Brady let out a snort of a laugh and suggested they begin hiking back to the forest's edge.

As the two adventure seekers began their journey back to the start, the forest suddenly fell silent. The birds stopped cawing, the insects quit buzzing, no leaves rustled in the wind, and not a single animal scurried on the forest floor. Then, with a load crack as if thick branches were being snapped in half like toothpicks, a creature slide down the dinizia tree the men just knocked against.

The men stared at the 8-foot-tall creature, lean with wooden limbs, spotted with green leaves. Its dark glowing eyes glared at the puny humans standing in front of it and then it let out a long groaning sound as if waking from a restful night's sleep.

Grady was the first to speak, "Oh. Shit." His eyes fixated on the forest giant; his body frozen in fear. That's when Brady noticed that behind the tree-man figure, where the massive dinizia tree was just towering above them, there was a huge empty spot.

Throughout the next five days, the men checked and re-checked all the materials from their research desperately trying to navigate the massive forest and locate the vanished dinizia tree to return the Woodlord back home. Over the course of that week, the Woodlord took great pleasure in teasing the men by stomping its huge wooden foot just a little too close or blowing a gust of wind through its hollowed mouth and knocking them into the surrounding trees. On one day, for no particular reason, the Woodlord swiped the land sending the men fifty feet across the forest floor. They begged and pleaded for the creature to stop, but to no avail. This was all a game for the evil beast.

On the sixth day, the men panicked while the sun began to set. The clock was running out and midnight was fast approaching. The best friends sobbed to each other, admitting they never thought this would turn out true, apologizing for bringing the other along. They attempted to get their bearings and prayed for a miracle.

Suddenly, as if appearing from thin air, Grady set his eyes on the missing dinizia tree. He checked his watch, 11:56 PM. They had four minutes to guide the Woodlord back to the tree and if they could outrun any tricks from the forest creature, there was a good chance of making it. The men took off, sprinting toward the massive tree just in their reach. Grady and Brady's wish had come true, they were finally scared for their lives, but they were still going to outrun death itself. They leapt over roots and leaves, and at 11:59 PM, the men sprung from the ground with outstretched arms towards the massive tree.

If a man is hanged in the forest and no one's around to hear it, does it make a sound?

IX

Tummy Aches

"Gah, my stomach has been in knots for three friggin' days!" Annie screamed at her roommate. She had paused next to the breakfast bar counter, leaning over bent knees, and holding onto the counter with one hand while the other pressed against her abdomen. Her face was strained from wincing for the millionth time today. Her roommate and friend, Gunner, watched from the sofa as her friend took a moment to suffer in pain.

"Maybe it's time to get it checked out."

A moment's pause, and then Annie took a deep breath. "I'll be fine, it'll pass soon enough." Not fully believing her own words, she asked, "Right?" Gunner pursed her lips and gave her eyebrows a quick arch before returning to the book she was reading. She knew her friend hated going to the doctor's office, but she also knew there was no point in putting up a fight about it.

That night, Gunner cooked up Annie's favorite dish – shrimp

alfredo with bowtie pasta – hoping to help cheer her friend up and distract her from the pain she'd been experiencing. The two women, both in their late twenties, enjoyed the meal paired with their favorite wines, red for Annie, white for Gunner. The pain from the morning's ordeal had seemed to subside. Annie was glad to feel normal again, Gunner was happy not hearing her friend moan and groan for a while. The two ate big bowls of pasta and shrimp and talked about the upcoming wedding plans.

"I still can't believe you're getting married." Gunner said with a mouthful of pasta. "It's surreal."

"I know, it feels kind of weird now that we've made it so far. But, when Gregg proposed something inside me just screamed 'yes,' so I screamed it, too."

"At least you're marrying the perfect man."

"Yeah..." Annie's breathy voice trailed as she pictured her perfect fiancé all dressed up in a tuxedo, waiting for her to walk down the aisle in her boho-inspired wedding dress, the light fabric waving against the light summer breeze. Gunner watched her friend daydreaming and rolled her eyes. It's not that she wasn't happy for Annie, but she couldn't help but feel a tinge of jealousy. Afterall, Gregg was Gunner's boyfriend before he was Annie's dream guy.

The wedding was set for next summer, which gave Annie nearly a year to plan. There were so many things to think about, but she was lucky to have her best friend and soon-to-be maid of honor by her side the whole way through. The girls decided to take a break from wedding planning for the weekend, though, and set off for a cottage-in-the-woods getaway. Gunner's uncle lent his cottage to the girls for the weekend, and neither of them could wait to get out to the woods to hike, sunbathe by the lake, swim in the crystal-clear water, and enjoy some much-needed relaxation.

Annie loved the cottage but hated the animal decorations plastered across the walls. Gunner's uncle was an avid hunter and would stuff his best kills to showcase them on the trophy wall. It never phased Gunner, she rather liked the thought of having a prized possession mounted for all to see, to bask in the memory of a successful and well-earned kill.

The girls quickly set out to swim in the cool lake under the summer's heat lamp that was the sun. Annie was the first to climb onto the wood dock and lay out under the sun's warming light. After Gunner left the water, she offered to run back to the cottage and return with wine. The women sipped their wine, chatted amongst themselves, and enjoyed the warm afternoon. However, it wasn't long before the good times ran out.

Before long, Annie was curled into a tight ball holding her stomach, retching from pain. Her stomach aches had returned and began ruining her girl's getaway with Gunner.

"Seriously, let's get you to a doctor. There's one in town, it's not a hospital." Gunner suggested.

Through gritted teeth and clenched eyes, Annie growled, "Nooo." A few moments later the pain had once again subsided, and the women were back to enjoying the late afternoon's warm breeze before it cooled for the night.

After the sun had set, the girls watched a cheesy horror flick, and the popcorn bowl had been emptied, they decided it was time for bed. Annie realized she had left her phone out on the dock, so she told Gunner she was going to run and get it. Gunner watched her friend walk into the dense forest of trees between the cottage and the lake and disappear into the darkness.

Annie could hardly see three feet in front of her, the clouds were covering the moon, so the entire woods were darker than usual. She knew the path well enough to navigate back to the lake, but she heard something close behind her that made her spin around quickly. She scanned the area the best she could with her eyes opened wide but couldn't see anything other than dark trees. The crunching of twigs on the ground echoed between the trees, but Annie couldn't locate the source. Suddenly, and before she could react, something jumped straight at her from the dark and she screamed.

"Raaaah!" Gunner screamed and held her arms out in an attack stance.

"For fuck's sake, you scared the piss out of me!" Gunner laughed at her frightened friend, gloating in the successful scare. They walked together to the lake's dock to grab Annie's phone.

When she picked it up, she saw a text from Gregg that said, "When you gonna do it? Clearly the mercury chloride isn't working quick enough." She stared at the message in confusion and then showed her friend. Gunner read the text and let a long huff out through her nose as she pulled out a gun.

The next morning, Gunner stood in front of the trophy wall smiling ear to ear at the latest addition: Annie.

X

Dust Bunnies

Kricket stared in horror as his boyfriend was torn limb from limb by the devious creatures. Their sharp grey teeth tearing his flesh in chunks, the fluffy fur being matted with his blood. He tried to clench his eyes shut and cover his ears, but the sticky, gooey sound of his muscles being ripped away from the bones they surrounded penetrated the barrier of his hands. The filthy terrifying creatures kept coming from underneath the couch like an army of puffballs coated in dust, hair, and crumbs. His mother warned him that letting dust bunnies collect would cause issues, but he never imagined they'd turn into feral, blood-thirsty beasts.

Pete and Kricket moved in together after nearly five months of dating. At 20- and 22-years-old, neither had much experience with what truly went into keeping a house tidy, but they picked out a rental and hoped for the best. When Kricket's mom visited after the boys had settled, she made some suggestions about the cleaning the bathroom which already had urine around the toilet, and shower scum building in the corner; she helped point out where dust loves to hide by sliding a white paper towel under the couch and having it come out grey. She knew her son well enough to know that he wouldn't take it upon himself to keep up with house chores, so she tasked Pete – the more responsible one in her opinion – with keeping order to the house. "Letting too many dust bunnies gather will cause you trouble."

Over the next few weeks, the dishes stacked up in the kitchen sink attracting some gnats, the laundry collected in piles across the bedroom and laundry room floors, and the dust settled on shelves, windowsills, gaming consoles, and under the couch. One night while the couple were watching a movie on the couch, something tickled Pete's ankle and his leg twitched from the light touch.

"What's wrong?" Kricket asked.

"Nothing, just got a twitch in the foot." And they continued watching the movie. A few minutes later, another sensation sent Pete's leg flying up again. This time, though, he let out an audible "ah." He pulled his knee up and rubbed his ankle, something had stung or bitten his foot. When he looked at his hand, he saw a dribble of blood smeared across the fingertips. It wasn't an alarming amount, but clearly something was hiding under the couch. Afraid it was a mouse, he jumped up and told Kricket to get off the couch. Together, they shoved the couch to the side, watching for anything to scurry from underneath it but all they found was some dust, a penny, and one of Pete's drawing pencils.

Kricket gave Pete a look that begged, "Are you going crazy?" But he rolled his eyes and started shoving the couch back in place. They returned to their positions on the couch, with Pete folding his legs up, and finished the rest of the movie. Soon after the end, the pair checked the doors to ensure they were locked and went to bed.

That night, Kricket woke to a strange sound filling the room. He leaned on his elbows and listened, picking up the sound of fairly high-pitched grumblings. The sound was unfamiliar, it wasn't the usual song of the neighborhood's stray cats, and it wasn't the chatter of field mice, it was something crossed between hyena's laugh mixed with the squeakiness that comes from sucking in helium. He sat up in the bed, and bumped Pete with his arm in an attempt to wake him, but unlike Kricket, Pete was a heavy sleeper. He whispered to himself, "You're no help." Kricket rolled to the side of the bed and lowered his feet slowly, not sure where the sound was coming from. He didn't want to make any sudden movements or much noise in case there was an intruder. He sat at the bed's edge for a moment, the soles of his feet spreading on the cool hardwood floor and listened to the odd squeals.

Kricket began taking slow steps out of the bedroom and down the hall, the noise was growing louder as he made his way toward the living room. The house was nearly pitch-black save for the areas the moonlight shone through the windows and illuminated the couple's furniture in a ghostly blue hue. He continued into the living room where the peculiar sound climaxed, the squeaks were bouncing off every inch of the living room. Kricket stood in the archway and stared around, attempting to locate the source of the sound. That's when he noticed something wriggling on the floor near the sofa. He crouched forward to get a clearer view, but still couldn't make out what was on the floor. A mouse? Or mice?

He lowered himself to the floor on his stomach which led him to scream for Pete.

Staring back at Kricket from three feet away and under the couch were hundreds of dark yellow eyes belonging to snarling fuzzy creatures, all scurrying about in the shadow of the sofa. Kricket screamed for Pete again who jolted from the bed and came rushing into the room. He turned the light on, searching the room quickly for his terrified boyfriend and upon seeing him lying on the floor, dropped to meet him.

"What?! What's wrong? Why are you on the floor?" His voice was frantic, his eyes were scanning the room for danger, he was confused and still in a sleepy daze. Kricket's eyes were frozen open staring at the demonic creatures with their sharp fangs more visible now with the light on. Pete lowered himself to investigate what was hiding under the couch and gasped sharply when he saw the same scene as Kricket.

Suddenly, like a wave of ocean water rushing to the shore, the creatures stormed from under the couch directly toward Pete and locked their jagged teeth into his body. Kricket curled into a ball against the wall screaming in agony.

XI

Charlie

Charlie had a curious nature about him, always exploring the town's darkest corners, investigating off-road paths, and taking things apart to understand how they worked. He didn't learn things the way other kids his age did through typical schoolwork or reading; he took a hands-on approach to life, and it taught him many things.

One afternoon he went to the woods behind his home, with his mother working late, Charlie knew he had some spare time for a quick adventure. He'd walked the wooden area a thousand times, familiarizing himself with the layout. He navigated the woods the way most children his age, ten-years-old, memorized video game levels, a combination of practice and muscle memory. He knew where the poison ivy patches were, could spin around fifty times and still know which direction to return home, and he always knew how many steps it'd take between entering and exiting the forest. Charlie went to the woods in search of an adventure, and what he found changed him forever.

Nearly halfway through the woods and sixty paces due east, there was a small creek that flowed between the trees. Following the water upstream led to a rocky formation with an entrance to a cave. Charlie had yet to explore the cave, so he marched to the entrance and tossed a stone in and waited. When nothing stirred or came barreling out of the dark cave, he decided it was safe enough to enter. His first few steps were quick, but as the darkness closed in around him, they grew slower, cautious, hesitant.

Around his feet were discarded trash items; beer cans, takeout boxes, wrappers, rotting food. Someone had been here; someone may live here. He looked around the area using a small flashlight he brought, there wasn't much to see. Charlie guessed that teenagers had been out here and left their garbage all over, he kicked a can out of his path and the echo bounced off the dark, stone walls. He continued further into the cave, careful of his step.

A few feet deeper into the darkness, Charlie's flashlight illuminated what he thought was a pile of clothes wadded against the wall. He moved towards the dirty clothing and suddenly the smell of filth and sewage filled his nostrils. His face twisted in disgust, he held a hand over his mouth and nose to alleviate some of the foul stench, but it still invaded his senses. Charlie approached the pile of clothes, but the intrusive odor got the best of him.

The smell bothered Charlie so much that he backed away and made off for home. He ran through the scattered trees and burst into the back door of his house. He rushed into the bathroom and began washing his face with soap and water just to get the smell of grim and decay clear from his nose. When Charlie's mother finished working and came out of her home office, she asked where he had been. Charlie replied he went exploring the woods again but didn't find anything new.

The next day was Saturday, the weekend was finally here which meant Charlie could explore the world around him all day long. He loaded a backpack up with some supplies, snacks, and juice, and hollered to his mom that he was heading to the woods.

"Be back before sundown." she shouted in return as she began reviewing recent order requests for her side business of personalized items.

Charlie navigated straight to the cave, ready to investigate the unexplored area more. He brought a larger, brighter flashlight and when he clicked it on, it fully illuminated the cave. He looked all around him, the dirty stone walls were covered with markings, rudimentary drawings, and words that didn't seem to make any logical sentences. He pressed on, kicking the trash along the ground out of his way as he stepped deeper into the cave to where the dirty clothes were.

The smell had resurfaced and began intruding on his senses again, but he came prepared. He grabbed a tube of lotion from his backpack and dabbed his upper lip just under his nose with it to help block the unpleasant stench. Once again, Charlie approached the pile of clothes, but with the brighter light he could see there was more than just a dirty clothes mound. He had stumbled upon a man, wrinkled with age, a dirty face hidden behind a tangled brown and grey straggly beard. For a moment, Charlie felt a tinge of fright, but he scanned over the body and realized it wasn't moving. He had found a dead man.

Charlie dropped his backpack and pulled out a pair of gloves, he didn't want to touch anything that might dirty his hands. He walked over to the body and tugged at its right shoulder, rolling the man from his side to his back. Charlie stood over the man and stared in astonishment; he'd never seen a dead body before. The smell was terrible, but the sight was strangely exhilarating. Charlie pulled at the filthy rags that covered the man, they nearly tore to shreds with little effort. He wondered how this man got here. Was he homeless? Or did he run away from someone? Charlie loved a good mystery.

He began poking the body here and there, examining the man's dirty feet which were scattered with cuts, his toes decorated with disgusting yellowing nails. He looked over his face closely, taking in all the deep wrinkles and greasy yet dry hair. His nose was bulbous, eyes were sunk in, and there were bugs in his hair. Charlie jerked backward from the man lying in filth, suddenly startled.

The man opened his pale blue eyes and stared right at Charlie. His mouth trembled open, and he spoke, "Please... help... me..." His words came out like hisses and reeked of decay.

Charlie's bright, youthful face smiled down on the man and he responded, "Not yet. I've never taken a human apart before."

XII

Floaters

I hate closing my eyes longer than a blink, not because I'm scared of the dark or because I'm afraid I'll miss out on something exciting or anything dumb like that. No, I hate closing my eyes because that's when the monsters come to life. They live in my eyes, and I can see them every time my lids cover my eyes. No one believes me, and it's getting increasingly worse. I even made an appointment with the optometrist who told me they were just floaters and that everyone has them. False! They're not floaters, and everyone does *not* have these monsters.

My best friend, Kik, told me all about this underwater haunted house last fall and we decided to take a road trip to visit it. We love haunted houses and had never been to – or even heard of – an underwater one. We packed the car full of snacks, swim trunks, and all the things we needed for a trip and headed out for the opening weekend. It was a 7.5-hour drive from our sleepy town of Milford, Delaware to the haunted city of Wilmington, North Carolina, but driving for hours didn't bother me in the least.

On the way down, we let our imaginations run wild with speculations of what we would see at the underwater attraction. "Maybe they'll have zombie mermaids or something like a kraken that chases you through a cave." I guessed enthusiastically.

"Oh man, that'd be sweet! What if there's like hallways you have to get through and find doors with air supplies before you drown?"

We both laughed, but I said, "I doubt they're going to risk people drowning."

The drive went quickly with our combined focus on all the excitement from this unique experience we were about to embark on. We checked into the hotel for the weekend, and asked the front desk woman if she knew anything about the haunted house attraction. She appeared physically upset, said she didn't know anything, and hurried off to the backroom where we couldn't see her. Sure, that was odd, but some people just don't like being scared. Kik and I love the rush a good scare gives us.

That night, we navigated our way to the attraction, The Dead Sea: An Underwater Haunting. The place was wicked with walls that looked like dark coral reefs, posters of famous underwater monsters like the one from *Creature from the Black Lagoon*, adaptations of the kraken, the shark from *Jaws*, and a bunch of others. There were flashing colored lights everywhere to illuminate mermaids, anglerfish, and creepy creatures. There were even sounds of waves crashing against the shore, bubbles, and whale songs. It was amazing, but through all the peacocking I noticed a very clear absence of one thing in particular – people. There was no one else in the building other than us. The ticket kiosk in the front lobby didn't have a worker standing by, and there wasn't anyone to collect our tickets.

We found a hallway with a sign posted that read: ENTER HERE. We began walking down the darkened hall which led to a huge room, similar to the lobby with dark rock walls like an underwater reef. The door clicked closed behind us and a whirring sound followed. Suddenly a loud buzzer rang out and filled the room with a horrid noise, we both flinched, and I covered my ears while I looked around the room. Kik looked at me with some panic in his eyes, but I just shrugged not knowing what was happening. The buzzing noise had stopped and then we heard a sound of rushing water, assuming it was a soundtrack like in the lobby, but I quickly realized it wasn't just another sound effect.

There were six grated pipes built into the walls that were dumping out water into the room, and before we knew it, the icy water had reached our shoes and started rising quickly.

"What the hell?" I screamed.

"What's happening? I-is this supposed to happen?"

Kik and I ran to the door through the quickly rising water, and shoved against it, but it was locked, bolted shut. The whirring noise must have been a waterproofing lock to contain the water to the room. Before long, the water was up to our waists and still rising. Panic began to sink in, and we both screamed for help. I kept telling myself this was part of the experience, but without any warning it was hard to believe it. Another twenty minutes, and we were fully swimming in the room. The floor was nearly five feet below us, but the drains continued to empty gallons of water into the decorated room.

After nearly an hour, the room was completely full of water with a small six-inch gap of air left at the top, just enough for us to suck in a breath before submerging again. I swam to each of the drains, pulling desperately at the grate to find a way out, but to no avail. As I swam back to the surface, I could see a hole open in the ceiling. As soon as it opened, a weird off-white colored stream came crashing down into the water, it reminded me of tapioca pudding, yellowish with tiny chunks. When the substance hit the water, the little chunks dispersed and swam in every direction, wiggling through the water like some weird shrimp-like creature. The microorganisms created a cloud between me and the surface, but my oxygen was running low, so I pushed up and burst through for another breath.

I could feel the strange creatures wriggling on my face, digging their way into the corners of my eyes, swimming over my cornea and forcing me to rapidly blink. I tried closing my eyes, but when I did, I saw a million little monsters with deep blue glowing eyes and tiny mouths filled with viciously sharp teeth. The micro-monsters had conquered my eyeballs and now continue to haunt my dreams.

XIII

Foresight

The woman's white and teal tennis shoe was caught in between the rotting wood that made up the old railroad. She had passed over it a thousand times on her daily morning jog, but today it wouldn't let go of her. Panic set in as she heard the whistle blow in the distance, closing in on her quickly. The freight train rounded the curve and fell into her direct line of sight, her eyes widened with terror. "No, no, shit!" She screamed out, desperately trying to untie her trapped shoe. The train was approaching, the wave of thunder through the metal and wood tracks rumbled through her body. The desperate woman yanked at her foot, attempting to discard the shoe and escape but it wouldn't let her loose. She looked up and saw the train's headlamp growing as it neared her. A blood-curdling scream escaped her body as the train's engine slammed into her delicate body and she burst into an explosion of blood, fleshy chunks, and shattering bones. The train passed as the shoe lay in between the broken wooden tracks.

A beautiful summer day with a warm breeze, bright sun, blue sky dotted with puffy white clouds, and a boy enjoying his favorite summertime activity – swimming. The pool was fairly crowded with it being such a magnificent day, but he didn't mind sharing the cool water with his friends and neighbors. He watched as a group of older boys took turns showing off, daring each other to twist and tumble during their dives. One of the boys caught him staring and dared him to dive from the high board. Not wanting to be teased, he agreed and made his way up the tall ladder past the low and mid boards. He stood toward the edge of the high board and took a gulping breath. Bounced once, twice, and forced himself forward. He dove down and opened his eyes just in time to see he miscalculated and was headed for the edge of the pool. A woman's shriek echoed over all the other sounds as the boy's head smashed against the hard tiled pool edge, spraying a sunburst of blood across the pavement before his limp body tumbled into the water. The boy's blood spread in the water in a quickly growing blob of red as onlookers stood motionless in horror.

An old woman, nearing her ninetieth year of life, lay in a hospital bed listening to a soothing tune from when she was younger. The music helped her stay focused, alert, but even with the familiar tune she knew her memory was fading. There had been falls, bruises, torn skin, aching muscles, cracking bones, and infections in these last few years, but she tried to keep a pleasant outlook. The nurse came in as she was drifting off to sleep. As she lolled her head to the side, her eyes fluttered in fear as the nurse suspiciously pulled a syringe from her pocket and inserted into a tube connected to the woman. Her eyes flared as she watched a single air bubble glide through the tube and just when she lost sight of it, her body convulsed. A pain like a lightning bolt ran through her body, her eyes went wild, and she could hear the machines beeping like a million car alarms. The old woman's body trembled as her organs began shutting down one by one as if someone began flicking circuit breakers. With one last piercing pain, the woman let out her last breath.

The man looked over the gorgeous mountain range from the edge of the vigorous hiking path he had just conquered with his wife, pleased at the reward for their efforts. The crisp, cool air filled his lungs with natural oxygen filtered from the forest of trees. The sun was to set in just a few more minutes, and the man felt an abundance of joy knowing the hiking trip brought him and his wife closer. He felt like it was helping them mend their relationship, create a stronger bond. They had begun to drift apart, but this trip had pulled them closer as they had to rely on each other to scale rock walls, disinfect cuts from thorn bushes, and push each other when they felt weak. He could hear her footsteps approaching him; he was ready to hold her hand and share in their victory. He felt her hands slide over his shoulders and down his back, a loving embrace sure to follow. Instead, a strong, quick jab against his sweating back jostled him forward and he disappeared over the cliff's edge. His body tossed against the jagged rocks like a wooden raft against the raging waters. His bones cracked, his face scraped against the rough terrain leaving bloody imprints of impact, he screamed but it was quickly hushed from a rock slamming into his side. He tumbled further and further until he landed cracked in half over a jagged termite hill sticking up.

Raven didn't like knowing how people would die, she never wanted to have the ability. She learned to wear gloves and keep her skin hidden behind fabrics, long sleeved shirts, pants, scarves, and hats. Any skin-on-skin contact was like an instant film flickering in her mind. Her eyes would flutter and roll back as she was forced to witness whatever horrible death awaited the person who touched her.

She shook her new manager's hand after she was hired on the spot and bore witness to the train accident that would claim her next week. Her neighbor's son's hand softly brushed her own as she handed him the runaway beachball, and she was forced to see his tragic demise. Her grandmother grabbed her wrist, when she visited, to say thank you for the company and the devilish nurse flashed in her mind. When her husband kissed her on their wedding day, she knew that one day would come when he'd invite her on a hike to the mountains.

About the Author

Goe is a simple guy who likes simple things like cheesecake, indie horror movies, weird sounds, and furniture shaped like food. He's born of Ohio blood but tends to bleed Tennessee whiskey. One day he decided he wanted to write a bunch of little horror stories, so after a bunch of backspacing and frowny faces he landed on these 13. Goe shoved them all together in a book and published it himself with the help of the onlines, and now you just read it. Unless you read this section first which, in that case, you're probably bad at reading books. Go to the beginning and start there, it's way better content than this section.

Printed by Libri Plureos GmbH in Hamburg, Germany